THE
EXTRA
POINT

THE
EXTRA
POINT

CHRIS KREIE

darbycreek
MINNEAPOLIS

Darby Creek
A division of Lerner Publishing Group, Inc.
241 First Avenue North
Minneapolis, MN 55401 USA

For reading levels and more information, look up this title at www.lernerbooks.com.

Cover and interior images: © pattern line/Shutterstock.com (scratch texture); © Eky Studio/Shutterstock.com (metal bolts); © Kriangsak Osvapoositkul/Shutterstock.com (rust texture); © iStockphoto.com/3bugsmom (player).

Main body text set in Janson Text LT Std 12/17.5.
Typeface provided by Adobe Systems.

Library of Congress Cataloging-in-Publication Data

The Cataloging-in-Publication Data for *The Extra Point* is on file at the Library of Congress.
ISBN 978-1-5124-3981-6 (lib. bdg.)
ISBN 978-1-5124-5353-9 (pbk.)
ISBN 978-1-5124-4870-2 (EB pdf)

Manufactured in the United States of America
1-42230-25779-3/28/2017

To Pat, a fierce advocate for libraries,
literacy, and the joy of life-long reading.
And a football fan too!

Chapter 1

Riley Carpenter walked along the running track that surrounded the football field. She picked her way through a crowd of students and fans who were here for the same reason she was: it was game night. The Renegades were about to play the Central Rams in their first game of the fall football season.

It was a good night for a game. The sun was an orange ball hanging low on the horizon, and there was a slight chill in the air.

As Riley headed toward the bleachers, the players on the field were going through pregame drills. The captains barked out orders and the rest of the players jumped and spun and rolled on the ground. Riley let out a chuckle. She knew the game well, coming from a football family. Her dad coached youth ball and both of her older brothers were star players. She loved the sport, but parts of it definitely looked silly.

"Riley! Up here!" She spotted her best friend Aisha shouting down to her from the sea of faces in the bleachers.

Riley bounded up the steps to their usual spot. Riley and Aisha had been going to Renegades games since before they were even in high school. "First game of the season!" she said. The two of them hugged. They had been best friends since they were put on the same soccer and basketball teams in elementary school.

"Senior year!" Aisha said. "I can't believe it."

"Me either!" Riley looked out at the field. "Our last chance to get to the state championship." The girls remained standing as the pep band played the Star Spangled Banner. When the anthem was over, the crowd cheered and everyone sat down. Riley looked at the scarf covering Aisha's head. "I love your hijab. Is it new?"

"Oh, thanks." Aisha touched the smooth red and black scarf. "Yeah, it's new. I thought I'd get into the school spirit. You know, Renegades Red."

One of the refs blew a whistle, and both girls turned to the field as the game began. Chava Gutierrez, the Renegades' quarterback, kicked off to the visiting Central Rams. "Since when is Chava the kicker?" asked Riley. "He didn't kick last season."

"Beats me," Aisha replied with a shrug.

Chava's kick was pathetically short, giving the Rams excellent field position near the fifty yard line.

The Rams made one good play after another. On the final play of the drive, the quarterback rolled to his right and threw a beautiful pass to one of his tight ends. The receiver jumped up high and snatched the ball out of the air. Once on the ground, he wrestled two more defenders and bullied his way into the end zone. Riley and Aisha groaned.

The Renegades tried to fire back. Chava threw a deep pass down the middle to wide receiver Anthony Barber, and another in the flat to running back Eddie Williams, which turned into a thirty-yard run. But the Renegades just couldn't get any points on the board.

By the end of the first quarter, the Rams were up 14–0. Finally, halfway through the second quarter, the Renegades responded in a brilliant play. It was fourth down on the Rams' five yard line when Chava faked a handoff to Eddie and went charging down the field. He sprinted around the outside for a touchdown. The crowd went nuts.

But the Renegades weren't able to keep up the momentum. Chava was unsuccessful on the extra point attempt and once again failed miserably on the kickoff. As he swung his kicking leg toward the ball, he almost whiffed—striking just the top part of the ball. The football took a few bounces and traveled only fifteen yards. A Rams player dove on top of it.

"Did he do that on purpose?" asked Aisha.

"I don't think so," said Riley.

"Why is Chava kicking anyway?" Aisha wondered out loud. "He's a great quarterback, but clearly when it comes to kicking, well . . . he stinks."

"I don't know," said Riley. "Colin Josephson was a senior last year, so with Colin gone I guess Chava is the best we've got now."

"It could be a long season."

The Rams set up for the next play. They snapped the ball, but the Renegades' star linebacker, Sean Coughlin, blitzed the quarterback up the middle and met him a split second after he took the snap. The quarterback never knew what hit him and went crashing to the turf. The ball flew from his hands and a Renegades defender pounced on it. Riley and Aisha jumped to their feet as Sean and the rest of the Renegades players celebrated the fumble recovery.

Sean's play was just what the Renegades needed to turn the game around. The crowd watched eagerly as they took possession of the ball and scored. By halftime the game was looking up for the Renegades.

"You excited for *our* game on Monday?" asked Aisha as the pep band streamed onto the field for their halftime performance.

"Of course," Riley said. "I just wish I knew if I'll be playing varsity or JV." Last season Riley had played on the JV soccer team, while Aisha was one of the stars on varsity.

"You'll make varsity," said Aisha. "You've improved so much from last year."

"Then why hasn't Coach given me a spot yet?" Riley asked. "What's she waiting for?"

Coach Bryant had named twenty girls to the varsity roster earlier in the week, but said she needed to evaluate the last few players a bit more before she could fill out the entire team. There were just two spots left and only one practice for Riley to show that she deserved one of them. Tomorrow's practice was make-it-or-break-it time before their first game on Monday.

"Don't sweat it," said Aisha. "You're going to make the team. With you kicking corners and me heading them in, we'll be a deadly combination."

Riley laughed, thinking back to how much time the two of them had spent practicing just that routine when they were younger. "Remember the one summer we went to the field every night to practice?"

Aisha chuckled. "Yeah, what were we, twelve? I remember being so bad and you spending every day for three weeks helping me with my ball handling, even after I had said I wanted to quit at least a dozen times."

The two friends smiled at each other. "Well, it clearly turned out all right," Riley said to Aisha. "I told you, all you needed was a little more practice, and now you're about to dominate in our senior season."

"*We're* about to dominate," Aisha corrected her.

Their conversation came to an end as the second half got underway. Riley had never been able to focus on much more than the game when she was watching football—she got swept up in the excitement on the field.

The Renegades kept it rolling in the second half, and everyone in the crowd, especially

Riley, showed their enthusiasm. With every first down, Riley felt the rush of it all—almost as if she were out there herself. The Renegades went on to beat the Rams 22–20.

Chapter
2

Riley raced down the soccer field chasing
Izzy Malone. Izzy was streaking down the
sideline in front of her, looking for a pass from
her teammate. Riley was trying to defend
Izzy but wasn't having much luck. It was
Saturday morning and Riley's last chance to
prove she was worthy of a varsity spot. She
was scrambling to do everything she could to
earn it.

Riley put her head down and summoned
every ounce of energy still left in her burning
legs, but it was no use. Izzy was fast—faster
than she was. At that point all Riley could hope

for was that Izzy wouldn't get the pass or that the ball would be behind her, allowing Riley a chance to catch up.

Unfortunately, neither of those things happened. Izzy took the pass from a teammate in full stride, touched it two or three times with her toes, and then drilled it into the box with the side of her foot. It was a perfect assist. Nidhi Patel one-timed the ball hard into the back of the net. She threw her arms into the air and jumped into a bear hug from Izzy and her other teammates.

"Carpenter! You need to stay on her. That goal's on you, Riley!" It was Coach Bryant, barking from the middle of the field.

"I know, Coach! My bad!" Riley hunched over with her hands on her knees, sucking in every last breath she could. Sweat dripped off her forehead onto the grass at her feet. She was exhausted.

"Okay, girls!" yelled Coach Bryant. "Bring it in!"

Riley stood tall and jogged toward the center circle along with the rest of the team.

"Good try," said Aisha. She handed Riley a water bottle. "Izzy's tough. But you're looking good out there."

Riley took a long swig from the bottle. "We'll see if it's good enough."

"Good practice, ladies," said the coach. "I'm excited for our chances this year, but just like any other year, nothing's going to come easy. We need to keep working hard and pushing ourselves all season long. You know my motto: some teams might beat us, but no one will ever out-hustle us."

Everyone, including Riley, cheered.

"I like the enthusiasm," said Coach Bryant, smiling. "But now comes the serious part. I can only take twenty-two girls on the varsity team. I wish I could take more than that, but, according to league rules, I can't. And as you know, I've already awarded twenty of those spots. This means there are only two spots left." She pulled out the clipboard she'd been cradling under her arm. "There's no easy way to do this, so I'm just going to do it."

Riley felt a giant lump in her throat. It

seemed like time stood still while she waited for Coach Bryant to say the names.

Coach continued, "The final varsity spots go to Izzy Malone and Te'Keya James. Congratulations, girls."

Izzy and Te'Keya shared a hug while the rest of the girls applauded. The news hit Riley like a truck. That was it. Her dreams of playing varsity soccer for the Renegades were over in the blink of an eye. Aisha wrapped her arm around Riley.

"All right, girls," said Coach Bryant. "Practice is over. Get some rest this weekend and be ready to play your best on Monday."

The team scattered, some walking toward the school, others running to the corners of the field, collecting equipment.

"You okay?" Aisha asked.

Riley nodded. "I wanted it. I wanted it bad." She tried to hold back tears.

"I know you did." Aisha grabbed her in a full hug. "I wanted it too. Not for you, though, for me. You were going to make me look good this year."

They both laughed. Riley pulled back and smacked Aisha on the shoulder. "So selfish," she joked.

"I'm just messing with you," said Aisha. "This totally sucks."

Riley blinked the tears from her eyes. "I guess I'll just have to be the best player the Renegades JV team has ever seen."

"That's the spirit. Glass half full, right?" Aisha motioned toward to the school. "Let's go. I'll buy you a bag of chips. Hot cheddar. Your favorite."

The two began walking arm in arm to the locker room.

"Carpenter!" Riley turned around. It was Coach Bryant.

"Yeah, Coach?" she said.

"Can I talk to you for a minute?"

"I'll catch up to you inside," Riley said to Aisha. "You better have those chips waiting for me when I get there."

"You got it!" Aisha ran to catch up with some other players.

Riley walked over to her coach. "What's up?"

Coach Bryant had a serious look on her face. "I have something else I need to tell you," she said. "And I hope you know this isn't easy for me."

Riley was confused. *What was she talking about?*

"I'm not putting you on JV."

"What?"

Coach wasn't making any sense.

"I wish I could find room for you this year," Coach Bryant said. "I really do. Your corner kick is stronger than anyone's. But you just don't have the speed to play varsity, and we don't have the room for you on JV. This program is really beginning to grow. We have an insane amount of young talent coming up. I need to open up spots on JV to freshman and sophomores so they can fine-tune their game and be ready to play varsity next season. It's important that I plan for the future. I need to make the team competitive enough to make it to the state championship. That's always been my goal."

Riley couldn't believe what she was hearing.

Just like that, Coach Bryant had put an end to her entire high school soccer career.

"You understand what I'm saying, I'm sure," said Coach.

"I understand," Riley responded. But she really didn't. She had devoted over ten years of her life to soccer, all with the dream of one day playing for the varsity team. She'd worked hard and done everything her coaches had ever asked her to do. She deserved a spot. At least a spot on JV. She'd earned it. Riley couldn't wrap her head around how this could have happened.

"We could use you as a student manager," said the coach.

Was she serious? Instead of playing the sport that she loved, Coach wanted her to gather balls and collect cones at the end of practices.

"Think about it." Coach Bryant patted her on the back. "You're a great kid, Riley. I'm sorry you won't be playing this year."

Riley just nodded.

"You good?" asked Coach.

"Yeah."

"All right then. I've got to get inside,"

Coach said. "Keep that manager spot in mind. You'd be a good one!" She turned and ran toward the school.

Riley was shocked. All she could do was stand there as still as a statue. She literally couldn't move.

Chapter
3

When she got home Riley made a beeline for her bedroom. She closed the door behind her and flopped down on her bed.

After a few minutes, Riley heard a knock on her door, but she didn't move.

Another knock—louder this time. "Riley, can I come in?" It was her dad's voice.

"I guess."

Her dad pushed open the door and stared at Riley sprawled out on top of her bed. "What's wrong?" he asked.

Riley couldn't quite make eye contact with him. She picked at some loose threads on her bedspread. "Coach cut me from the team. I won't even be playing JV."

Her dad sighed. "I'm so sorry, Riley. You must be really upset."

When Riley didn't respond, he paused a moment and then added, "I know it's a big deal right now, but in the long run—"

"I'll be fine, Dad," Riley cut in. "I just need my space."

"Okay." Her dad nodded. "We'll give you the weekend. After that you need to pick yourself up and rejoin the land of the living." He stared intently at Riley, but when she still didn't look up, he left.

Riley knew her dad was right, but she wasn't in the mood for a pep talk. She didn't even want to think about the team right now. All she wanted was to be alone.

Riley stayed in her bedroom all weekend, and like her dad had promised, her parents didn't bother her.

Monday morning came, but Riley stayed in bed. After giving her a stern look, Riley's mom let her stay home from school. She seemed to understand that Riley needed a little more time.

Riley was relieved. It was game day for the soccer team and she knew the girls on her team—the team she hadn't made and would never play with again—would all be dressed up. The theme was "black out," and the team loved to go all-out for themed game days. Riley couldn't face being around the girls and feeling so left out. She'd go to school tomorrow. After the hype of the first game was over.

Eventually Riley dragged herself down to the living room to watch TV and half-heartedly do some of her homework. At 11:30 she finally broke down and checked her phone to see what Aisha and the other girls were up to. She scanned through the latest pictures Aisha had posted. There were lots of them, all with soccer players in goofy poses or with huge smiles on their faces decked out head to toe in black. Looking at the pictures wasn't as bad as Riley thought it was going to be. It actually felt good to see Aisha so happy. The team meant even more to Aisha than it did to her.

After a couple minutes of looking at images

other girls had posted, Riley noticed several identical statuses from some of her guy friends. She ignored them at first, but after seeing the same one over and over, she finally stopped on one of them to take a closer look.

All the posts were from members of the football team, and they were all advertising some kind of tryout later that afternoon. "Renegades football needs you," the message read. "If you can kick a ball and you want to be part of a winning team, come to open tryouts after school today and you can become the next Renegades placekicker. All guys are welcome. No football experience necessary."

Riley remembered back to last Friday's game and almost laughed. It wasn't hard to understand why the Renegades were looking for a new kicker. Chava had been pretty bad on Friday night. Even Riley herself could have done a better job than Chava had. It was clear that he had a great arm, but not such a great leg.

Which isn't surprising, Riley thought. *In soccer, some players are great at dribbling and footwork, while others just have a knack for finding the back of the net.* Her talent was corner kicks. Coach had always said she had the best leg on the team.

As she envisioned herself taking corner kicks, an idea bounced back and forth in Riley's mind. *I can't*, she thought. *Or can I?*

She pictured herself strapping on pads and a helmet and kicking field goals for the Renegades. *Why not try out? What's the worst that could happen?*

The more the idea grew in her head, the more she couldn't stop thinking about it. *I'm a good kicker*, she thought. *Why couldn't I kick a football? I can kick better than Chava, that's for sure. What's so crazy about that?*

She looked back at the posts that streamed on her newsfeed and let out a laugh. She reread part of it. "All guys are welcome," she smiled. *Guys, huh? We'll just have to see about that.*

Chapter 4

Riley drove up to the community football field at the park. She'd decided she should give this kicking idea a try before making a complete fool of herself in front of the team at tryouts. So back home she had raided the shed to collect her dad's youth league equipment bag, about ten balls, and a tee.

With her bag in tow, Riley walked along the twenty yard line toward the center of the field. The fear of seeing someone she knew— or running into a teacher who would question why she hadn't been in class today—had prompted her to go to this field instead of the one at the high school, but she was still a little paranoid that somebody might catch her.

Once she was satisfied that there was nobody else around, she dumped the bag at her feet, unzipped it, and pulled out a ball and a tee.

Riley placed the tee and the ball directly on the twenty. *Here goes nothing*, she thought as she took a few steps backward. Riley had watched enough football to know that almost all kickers use the side of their foot to blast the ball into the air. This meant they approached the ball from a diagonal direction, which was good for Riley because using the side of her foot was exactly what she did when she hit her deadly accurate corner kicks in soccer. The motion seemed almost identical.

Riley took a couple of deep breaths and an image of a perfect corner kick played in her mind: couple short steps then one long stride. Cock your kicking leg back, plant your other foot near the ball, then sweep your leg forward in a violent strike. Swing under and through the ball, resulting in a powerful kick that rises and bends through the air, dropping swiftly into the box at the feet of a fellow teammate.

She took a few more breaths and looked out at the very different kind of field in front of her. *Time to make it happen*, she thought. Riley charged toward the football, planted her left foot, and brought back her right. Then she swung her kicking leg with all her might toward the ball. She struck it hard. The ball sailed through the air. The kick had felt good. She had made solid contact. But as Riley watched, the ball hooked wildly to the left and didn't come anywhere near the goal posts.

Riley scrunched up her face, disappointed and confused.

She lined up another one and went through the same motion. Short steps toward the football, plant the foot, strike the ball hard with the side of her shoe. The end result was the same. The ball had good distance, but it missed the uprights by fifteen or twenty feet to the left.

A third ball and the same thing.

Suddenly it dawned on her: she'd trained all her life to bend a soccer ball. Bend it to make the ball first spin away from the goal but then ultimately curve back into the box and toward a waiting teammate.

Football kickers don't really bend the ball, she thought. *Sure they kick it with the side of their foot like soccer players do, but placekickers want the ball to travel straight.*

She set another ball on the tee and took three steps back and two steps to her left. *Kick it straight,* she thought to herself. *Swing the leg fast and kick the ball straight.*

Riley focused her eyes on the ball. She bent her body slightly toward the ground, then she rushed toward the ball.

Smack! Her leg blasted forward like a slingshot and her foot sent the ball sailing. End over end, the ball flew. Quietly and magically it split the uprights, clearing the crossbar by a good twenty feet. The kick was a thing of beauty. Riley's first-ever successful field goal.

"Yes!" she shouted. She pumped her fist above her. "Yes! Yes! Yes!" She had done it. She'd kicked a field goal. The only question was, could she do it again?

Riley lined up another kick, then another. She made six more attempts until all the balls from her bag were gone. Of those six kicks, she made three. Not great, but she felt like she was getting better. Every time she kicked the motion felt more natural, and she wasn't hooking the ball as much as she had at first.

Riley fished her phone from her pocket and checked the time. Two more hours before the open tryouts. That was plenty of time to hone her craft—to practice kicking and get good enough to beat out any guy who was planning to compete with her for the spot. She grabbed the ball bag and ran to collect the footballs.

Chapter 5

When Riley arrived at the high school, players from the football team were dressed in pads and practice uniforms. Some were stretching and jogging around on the field. Some were tossing a ball back and forth. Others were talking with coaches. Riley watched from the sideline for a few minutes then set down her bag and jogged onto the field. *Here goes nothing.*

The effect was immediate. Players stopped midstretch. The throwing came to an abrupt halt. The conversations and chatter all dropped away. It seemed as though the entire Renegades team was staring at her.

Riley ignored the players and ran toward a small group of boys dressed in shorts and T-shirts. She recognized several of them from the club soccer team that competed in the summer. She figured they were there for the same reason she was.

"Hey, Riley," said Aiden, one of the soccer players.

"What's up, Riley?" said Mustafa, another.

"Not much," she said.

"You here to kick?" asked Mustafa.

Riley just nodded, waiting for the taunting she was sure to follow.

"Cool," said Mustafa.

"That's awesome," said Aiden. "Good luck."

Riley smiled.

"Okay, fellas!" yelled a coach from the field. He motioned them over to join him at the fifteen yard line.

The boys and Riley jogged toward the coach. "All right, fellas," the coach said again but stopped midsentence. He looked directly at Riley. "This is kicking tryouts, young lady. You in the right place?"

"I'm in the right place," said Riley as confidently as she could. "I'm here to kick."

The coach pursed his lips and nodded. "All right," he said. "All right. Glad to have you."

Riley nodded back.

"I'm Coach Turner," he said. "And as far as I'm concerned, what's going to happen over the next half hour or so is as important as anything else this football team is going to do all year. If this tryout goes as I hope, one of you will join the Renegades and become an important piece of our team. This is serious business, so if any of you are here as a joke or to make a mockery of my team, you can leave right now."

Coach Turner scanned the group. His gaze stopped for several seconds on Riley. She held eye contact with him the entire time but didn't move from her spot.

"Okay then," he said. "Let's get to it. Line it up."

After Coach Turner gave them a crash course on the basics of kicking a football, Mustafa was first. A player from the football team crouched down next to the tee, holding the ball on its spot. Mustafa approached the ball and kicked. The football traveled straight, but never got more than about 10 feet off the ground. His kick wasn't even close. He walked away, shaking his head.

Aiden followed. Then the three other guys took their turns. One of them made a good attempt that was close to going through the uprights, but none of them kicked a successful field goal.

Riley was the last one to go. As she got ready for her attempt, a small group of players from the team wandered over.

"I thought cheerleading tryouts were last week," joked Sean Coughlin. Riley wasn't surprised. Everyone knew Sean was the star of the team and loved attention. He had been playing varsity since ninth grade and already had a big football scholarship lined up for next year. The only thing that surpassed Sean's football talent was his ego. "Sweetheart, this is a football tryout. Your legs are meant for jumps and high kicks, not field goals." He laughed along with a couple of his buddies.

Riley tried to lock in and ignore Sean, but her heart was racing. Way too many people were watching her.

She dug in and blasted the ball with all her strength.

It was a horrible kick. The ball sailed to the right and almost took out one of the assistant coaches. He had to duck to avoid getting smacked in the head.

"Nice kick," Sean snorted. He and his friends were doubled over in laughter. Riley's cheeks burned with anger and embarrassment. She knew she could do better.

"Next!" shouted Coach Turner.

Mustafa took his spot for his second attempt.

"Can I have another shot?" asked Riley.

"When it's your turn," Coach Turner replied gruffly.

Sean and his friends were still talking and snickering just a few feet away. It made Riley even more determined to nail an attempt.

"I was off on that one," she said. "I'd like another chance."

"You can kick when it's your turn to kick,"

Coach Turner repeated.

"It's okay," said Mustafa. "Riley can go."

"Okay, son." Coach Turner sighed. He turned to Riley. "I guess you're up again."

Riley nodded her thanks at Mustafa then looked at the coach. "Okay if I back it up a bit?"

Coach Turner shrugged. "It's your kick."

"Take it back to the thirty," said Riley to the player holding the ball.

"Ooh." A chorus rang out from the players watching. Riley walked backward. The rest of the group followed.

"That's a forty-yard field goal," said Coach Turner.

"I know," Riley replied. The farthest kick she had tried at the park was from the twenty-five yard line, officially a thirty-five-yard kick. But many of her kicks had cleared the crossbar easily. She figured she could do it from forty. She also figured that a kick from that distance would prove she meant business and would show Sean and his idiot friends that she wasn't going to back down so easily.

More players came over to join the group of spectators, including Chava. Riley wondered how he felt about being replaced as the kicker.

It seemed like everyone was watching.

Riley got into position. She breathed deeply. Her eyes locked on the ball. In a flash, she stepped forward, swung her leg, and kicked. The sound of her foot colliding with the ball was music to her ears. It was a sound she had heard before—the sound of a perfectly kicked ball.

Everyone watched as the ball soared high into the air, well over the crossbar and almost perfectly through the uprights. The kick was good.

The players around her cheered. Even the other guys who were there for the tryouts were impressed. Riley shot a glance at the only player who remained silent—Sean. Her view of him was quickly blocked by players gathering around her, congratulating her and patting her on the back.

"Excellent kick." Riley turned around. It was Chava.

"Thanks," she said.

"I hope you make the team," he said. "We'd be a good pair." Riley was confused, and her face must have showed it because Chava went on to explain, "I'm going to be the holder. For field goals and extra points."

"Oh . . . right," was all Riley could manage to respond.

Chava laughed. "Anyway, good luck."

"Okay, all of you," shouted Coach Turner. "Show's over! If you're not a kicker, get back to practice!"

The players dispersed and the kicking tryouts resumed. Riley made a few more kicks, but she couldn't get into a rhythm. It felt like for every kick she made, she missed another. Some were embarrassingly bad. But by the end, she'd made five successful kicks, which was exactly five more than the rest of the guys combined. The spot of Renegades kicker was hers.

Chapter 6

At dinner Riley told her parents about what she had done that day. After a short pause, her dad's face broke into a huge grin.

"I always figured my boys would follow in their old man's footsteps and play ball," he said between mouthfuls. "But you? My little girl? My little princess?" He winked at Riley.

"I haven't been your little princess since I gave up my tutu for a pair of soccer cleats on my fifth birthday," Riley said with a smile.

"Riley, how in the world are you ever going to tackle?" asked her mom.

Riley and her dad laughed. "I don't have to

tackle," said Riley. "I'm the kicker. I just come in for field goals and extra points."

"You might have to tackle on kickoffs," said her dad, "if the kick returner gets past all your teammates. You're the last line of defense to stop a return for a touchdown."

"I guess I hadn't thought of that," said Riley. She shrugged. "I can do it, though. I'm tough." She lifted both arms and flexed her biceps.

"That's my girl," her dad said.

"Your princess," joked Riley.

Riley grabbed a piece of bread and sopped up some remaining gravy from her plate. Her mom's look of concern softened and her dad beamed at her as she shoved the bread into her mouth. "Mind if I'm excused?" she asked. "I want to be rested for my first day of practice."

"You're excused," said her mom.

"Thanks for the awesome meal," said Riley, standing and grabbing her dishes.

Her mom smiled. "Anything I can do to help bulk up my new football player."

At school the next morning, most of her classmates had heard about Riley's new position. They congratulated her as she walked down the hallways. She was pumped about the thought of getting back out on the field.

It was the longest day of classes she could remember. Being part of a team was something Riley had always loved. Being part of this new team, with this new group of guys and playing a sport she'd only ever watched before, was especially exciting.

When the last bell of the day finally rang, Riley grabbed her backpack, blasted out of her seat, and headed straight to the girls' locker room. When she got there, members of the soccer and cross country teams were already getting ready for their practices.

Riley said hi to a few girls she knew and then looked around. Coach Turner had told her he would arrange for her practice uniform to be there waiting for her. She found it positioned neatly on a bench in front of a row of lockers. It was propped up perfectly like a display in a museum. She grabbed the short, white pants stuffed with pads and held them in front of her. *Cool.* Then she lifted up the black-and-white jersey wrapped tightly around a pair of shoulder pads. A giant number 2 was printed on the front and back.

"Hey there, football hero." It was Aisha.

"Hey!" They hugged. "Isn't this so weird?" said Riley.

"Weird but awesome," Aisha responded. "You're a warrior. You're going to dominate out there."

Riley snorted. "Let's not go overboard. I'm just hoping I don't screw up too much." She handed the shirt and shoulder pads to Aisha. "Make yourself useful, would you? I could use some help putting this stuff on."

The two of them pushed and pulled, stretched and grabbed at the equipment until all of it was successfully covering Riley. She stepped in front of the mirror, her helmet fit loosely on her head and the facemask partially blocked her view.

"How do I look?" she asked.

"Like a bobblehead," said Aisha.

"Thanks for the vote of confidence." She turned toward Aisha, grinning. "Well, I don't want to be late. Wish me luck."

Aisha patted her hard with two fists on top of her shoulder pads. "Good luck, soldier. Make it happen, girl!"

***

A few minutes later, Riley was out on the field going through warm-up drills led by Chava and another captain. The last drill had the players lunging down the field. It was exhausting, but not that different from the warm-ups she'd done hundreds of times with her soccer team. Still, she wasn't used to the routine. Riley began to fall behind.

"Too much for you, Carpenter?" Sean sneered.

Chava shot an angry look at Sean and then looked over his shoulder at Riley.

"No way!" she shot back. She picked up the pace.

"That's what I like to hear!" Chava yelled. "Welcome to the team, Rookie!"

Riley beamed behind her face mask. "Glad to be here!"

A whistle blew. It was Coach Turner. "Come on over, guys!" He was standing at the fifty yard line. Riley and the rest of the team raced over. "Take a knee!"

In unison, the team went down on one knee, circling their coach. Riley looked around and tried to get in the same position as all of the other players, casually draping her forearm on one of her legs.

"We've got some quick business to get out of the way," said Coach. "I want you all to welcome your new teammate, someone who's going to help us get some very important wins this season. Let's hear it for our new kicker, Riley Carpenter."

The players let out a chorus of hoots and hollers.

"Here's the deal," Coach Turner continued. "Riley's a girl. I'm sure you've figured that out by now." The players laughed. "But on this field and on my team we're all Renegades, and we all get the same treatment regardless of our gender."

Riley heard a snicker behind her. She looked over her shoulder to see Sean muttering under his breath.

The coach stopped his speech. "Something wrong, Carpenter?"

"No, Coach," said Riley. "Nothing's wrong. I'm ready to work hard."

"That's what I like to hear." Coach nodded.

Sean whispered something again. Riley heard him say her name. She clenched her teeth, trying her best to ignore him.

Coach continued, "You work hard out here, I'll reward you. You slack off, I'll get on your case—no matter which locker room you use. This is about winning games and becoming the best team we can possibly be, am I right?"

"Right!" shouted the team.

"All right then," said Coach. "Let's get started."

Riley grinned. This was the moment she had been waiting for.

Chapter

7

"Let's go, Aisha!" Riley stood alone in the bleachers after practice on Thursday, watching the soccer team take on the Hawks. "Go! Go!" Aisha had gotten ahead of the defenders and was running alone with the ball toward the opposing goalie. She did a quick stutter step, faked a shot, and froze the goalie. Then she easily dribbled to the right and had a wide open net. She tapped it gently with her foot and rolled the ball slowly into the goal.

"Yes!" shouted Riley.

The rest of the team rushed to Aisha to celebrate. The Renegades were leading the Hawks 3–0. Aisha waved to Riley in the stands.

It wasn't easy watching the game from the bleachers instead of on the field, but Riley had to focus on football now. And she was happy she had made it in time to see Aisha score her goal. Riley's third day of football practice had ended just a few minutes ago and she had sprinted to the soccer field to catch the last bit of the game. She hadn't even bothered to take off her practice uniform.

Except for Sean Coughlin, who continued his taunts and insults, the day had gone well. Riley's kicking had made small improvements, and she was building muscles in places she barely knew muscles even existed. Her favorite part was the kickoff. She would run up and just whack the ball as hard as she possibly could, watching it fly through the sky. Her best one so far had made it to the twenty yard line. She was doing pretty well, Coach Turner had told her, but it was Riley's goal to one day kick the ball into the end zone. That would take some practice and would mean adding strength to her leg, but she was determined to do it.

The referee blew the whistle and the game was over. The Renegades had won easily. After a short postgame talk from Coach Bryant, Aisha headed over to the stands and Riley climbed down the bleachers to meet her.

"Awesome goal," said Riley.

"Thanks." Aisha smiled. "Nice uniform."

Riley looked down at her football gear. "I didn't want to miss the game," she said.

"I'm just messing with you," Aisha said. The two of them headed toward the school.

"Big game tomorrow night," Aisha said. "You ready?"

"I think so," Riley said. "I'm excited, but nervous too. I just hope we win big so if I do miss some kicks it won't really matter."

"There's going to be a ton of people there. A group of us were talking about it at student council," said Aisha.

"That makes me feel better," said Riley with an exaggerated eye roll.

Aisha laughed. "They'll be there to see you. To support you. We've got your back."

They walked onto the football field and began heading for the door that leads to the girls' locker room.

"How are things going by the way?" asked Aisha. "Are you getting better at kicking?"

"Things are good," said Riley. "I'm doing okay. I'm still learning what works, though."

"You'll get the hang of it."

"Yeah," said Riley, feeling a little worried. She hadn't tried a new sport for a long time. She was so used to playing soccer almost all year round. Although she and Aisha played basketball too, that was only when the soccer fields were covered in too much snow or ice to practice on. And they had been doing it long enough that even going back to basketball after a long run of soccer wasn't as jarring anymore.

"Forget about it," said Aisha. "You're a great athlete. And you just started kicking a few days ago. Of course you're going to get better. It just takes time."

"I guess you're right," said Riley. "It's just hard starting from scratch."

"Coach Turner gave you the kicking spot for a reason," said Aisha. "He has confidence in you, so you should too."

Riley stopped in the middle of the field. "Hey, speaking of Coach, I told him I'd get in a few extra kicks after your game was over. I'll see you later."

"Want any help?" asked Aisha. "I don't know much about a football, but I could hold for you or whatever."

"No, I'm good. I've got everything I need." Riley appreciated the offer, but she really just needed the time to figure things out.

"Sounds good," said Aisha. "Thanks for coming."

"Wouldn't have missed it." They hugged. Then Riley headed off to collect some footballs and get to work.

Chapter 8

On game day, Riley sat on a bench in the
girls' locker room staring into a mirror. She
could hardly believe the girl staring back at
her. A girl dressed from head to toe in a crisp,
clean Renegades football uniform. So much
had happened during the last week. Never in
a million years would she have predicted that
she'd be sitting here, preparing to go kick for
the Renegades.

As she made her way onto the field, Riley
smelled the freshly painted white lines and her
heart skipped a beat. She felt the sponginess
of the soft turf below her feet and tried to

stay calm. Teammates swarmed around her and members of the band clanked their music stands together in the bleachers. She looked up at the lights that were illuminating the dusk of early evening.

"Game night is the best, don't you think?"

Riley turned. It was Chava.

"It's my first one," said Riley. She had played plenty of soccer games before, but those games never had an atmosphere that could match this.

"Still, you can feel it." Chava nodded. "Hey, let's get it done! Big win tonight?" He held out his fist.

Riley bumped it with hers. "Big win," she said, then watched Chava walk out to the middle of the field for the coin toss.

The Renegades got the ball first, which was a relief for Riley because it meant she didn't have to kick off right away. She hung back and watched her teammates take the field, trying to calm the butterflies in her stomach.

The Renegades' drive stalled out on their own forty yard line, resulting in a punt. Their opponent, the Bears from Jefferson High, fumbled the ball on their first play, giving the ball back to the Renegades in Bears' territory. Chava and the guys made the most of their opportunity. After two long runs, Chava drifted back to throw and dropped a perfect pass into the arms of receiver Anthony Barber. It was a thing of beauty—an easy touchdown.

Riley celebrated from her spot on the sideline and almost forgot that a Renegades touchdown meant she was up.

It was time for her to kick the extra point. She slapped on her helmet, grabbed the tee off the ground, and sprinted onto the field. Chava was waiting for her.

"Nice throw," she said.

"Thanks," he said as she handed him the tee. "Now let's get the point."

Riley suddenly realized the sound of the crowd was as loud as it had been all night, even louder than after the Renegades touchdown.

"What's going on?" Riley asked.

"They're cheering for you," said Chava. "Okay. Here we go. Get set."

Cheering for me? Riley thought. *But I haven't done anything yet.*

But now wasn't the time for her to bask in the glory. Her teammates were lining up and the play clock was ticking. She took three giant steps backward and then two sideways steps to her left. Her heart was pounding.

She focused on the tee, the spot where the ball would be in a matter of seconds. Chava barked out a couple of calls, then a split second later the football was sailing into his hands. Riley moved forward at the same time as Chava set the ball onto the tee. Riley dug her left foot into the ground and kicked her right leg forward.

Boom! She made solid contact. It felt great. But when she looked up she saw that the ball had missed by several feet to the right. The crowd let out a collective groan. Her first kick as a member of the Renegades and she had missed it. It was not how she had hoped her career would begin.

Chava patted her on the back. Several other players ran over to her and did the same.

"No worries," said Chava. "You'll get the next one." With that, some players ran off the field and others came on as the team prepared for the next play. Riley had no time to wallow in her disappointed. She had to prepare for the kickoff.

The kickoff went much better than her extra point. She laid solidly into the ball and drove it high and far toward the Bears' kick returner. He had to take a couple steps back to catch the ball. Moments later a whole cluster of Renegades players swarmed him, dragging him to the ground.

Riley grabbed the tee and began jogging off the field when suddenly she felt a hard blow to her shoulder. She stumbled a bit as one of her teammates bumped into her on his way out to the field. She assumed it was an accident, but when she turned to see that the player was Sean, she knew right away it was intentional. She watched him as he kept running, never looking back.

"Keep your head up," said Coach Turner. "Nice kickoff."

The rest of the first half went by quickly. Neither team scored any more points. With only a few seconds left in the half, and on third down, Chava threw an incomplete pass at the Jaguars thirty yard line. It was fourth down.

"Let's kick it!" yelled Coach.

Riley was shocked. This would be a long field goal attempt. Longer than any she had ever made.

"Give it your best," said Coach Turner.

Riley ran onto the field, and again the crowd gave her a loud reception. "Let's have some fun," said Chava. "This will be a forty-seven-yarder."

"This is ridiculous," said Riley. "I've never even tried to kick that far." Riley had definitely improved over her week of practice, but they had only worked on shorter, more manageable distances.

"Coach thinks you can," he said.

Riley shook her head but got into position all the same.

She took a quick look into the stands. Everyone was on their feet.

No pressure, she thought. *If I miss, my teammates will understand. No one really expects me to make this anyway.* The thought brought a huge smile to her face.

"Let's shock the world," she said out loud.

Chava called for the ball. He received the snap, Riley stepped toward him, he placed the ball down and Riley kicked it. *Bam!* The ball flew high and far. She and Chava stood and watched as it sailed closer and closer to the goal posts.

It had a chance. It really did.

The crowd was dead silent.

In the cool of the fall night, under the bright stadium lights, the ball went through the uprights and over the crossbar. It was good.

The stadium erupted. The guys on the line surrounded her. Riley raised both hands into the air.

"You did it!" yelled Chava.

"I did!" yelled Riley.

The clock ran out and the half was over. Back on the sidelines, her teammates whooped it up and showered her with slaps and high fives. She had made her first field goal, and it was a long one—longer than she ever even thought she could kick. But best of all, it had added to her team's lead. The Renegades were ahead at the half 9–0 over the Bears.

Chapter 9

Saturday morning things started to get really crazy. Riley slept late and woke up to her phone buzzing almost nonstop from all the messages she was getting. She thought they would just be congratulations for the team's 29–7 victory over the Bears, but it turned out that there was even bigger news. Apparently her forty-seven-yard field goal was a conference record. Coach had texted to congratulate her. She texted Aisha.

Riley: *Guess what? I set a conference record.*

Aisha: *I heard. So proud of you!*

Riley: *Coach said some local TV reporters are coming to practice Monday.*

Aisha: *Really? So awesome! You deserve it.*

Riley: *Thanks. I hope I don't make a complete fool out of myself.*

Aisha: *Of course you won't!*

When Monday's practice rolled around, Riley was greeted by a handful of TV reporters just like Coach had told her she would be.

"You've got two minutes," said Coach Turner. "Then we need you on the field."

Riley stepped up to the small group gathered at the fence.

"What's it like being the first girl to play football for the Renegades?" asked one of the reporters. Several cameras were pointed at her, and a few microphones were held in front in her face.

"I'm honored," said Riley. "But it's not about me being a girl. It's about me being a good kicker and helping my team."

"Tell us how you felt when you set the conference record," said another reporter.

"I didn't even know it was a record until the next day," she said. "It's pretty cool. But maybe I can break the new record too." She smiled.

The reporters laughed.

"And what about the reaction from your school and community?" asked someone else. "You must be getting a lot of attention because you're a young lady playing a traditionally guys' game."

Riley smiled. "Well, you all are here. That's something." More laughter from the reporters. "Seriously, though, it's been cool. My classmates and teachers have had my back. But like I said before, my job is to kick the ball and put points on the board. The fact that I'm a girl isn't that important in my book."

After a few more questions, Coach Turner cut in, "All right, hot shot! Paparazzi time's up!"

"Gotta listen to the coach," said Riley. "Thanks, everyone."

Riley ran toward where the guys were stretching and warming up for practice. Before she could take her spot in the group, Sean sprinted over to her.

She gritted her teeth. She was having such a good day, and she didn't want to let him spoil it for her.

"Think you're pretty big time, don't you?" he asked.

"Not really," she said. "I'm just doing my job. Kicking the ball just like you're tackling."

"All the fancy reporters seem to really love you," he said. "I say big deal. You made one field goal. I've been helping this team win games for over three seasons."

Riley thought back to seeing Sean being interviewed on TV the past few years. It had happened a couple of times a season since he started on varsity. He seemed to think the interviews were a big deal when they were about him. But Riley pushed the thought aside.

"You're right," said Riley. She didn't want to stoop to his level. She wanted to be the bigger person. "You're a great player. We can both help this team win."

"Everything okay over there?" It was Coach Turner.

"Yeah, Coach!" shouted Riley. "Just talking strategy."

Sean got in her face. "I'm the reason this team wins games," he said. "Me. Not you. That interview should have been mine."

"This is a team," Riley said. She bumped him as she walked away. "Everyone helps."

Riley got in the warm-ups line next to Chava. "You good?" he asked.

"Yep." But Riley couldn't quite shake what Sean had said.

***

That night Aisha and Riley hung out in Riley's living room and watched her interview on the local news.

"Can I have your autograph?" asked Aisha.

"Shut up," Riley shot back. The fact that she was receiving so much hype for making one long field goal was crazy. Ridiculous really. In a way, Sean was right. It did look like she was trying to be the new star— putting herself before the team.

She wondered what the other guys were thinking. They were the ones scoring the touchdowns, they were the ones playing tough defense. All she was doing was kicking. And she was missing just as many kicks as she was making. Riley felt huge pressure to get better.

Chapter

10

The Renegades played well the following week
and beat the Park Orioles in an away game.
Riley was getting used to the routine. Bus rides
were fun and most of the players had started
opening up to her and treating her like one of
them. They included her in their jokes and in
their smack talk.

At Park High School, Coach Turner had to
track down a custodian to get the girls' locker
rooms unlocked. Coach told him that Riley
was their secret weapon and that she needed
her own, private locker room. The custodian
seemed doubtful, but unlocked the door. Once

he left, Riley and Coach Turner both laughed about the whole thing.

The play of the game against Park was a near-perfect flea flicker. Chava took the snap from center and then retreated a couple of steps to hand the ball off to Eddie. Eddie sprinted hard toward the line of scrimmage, freezing the linebackers and safeties who had stepped up to stop the run.

Meanwhile, Anthony had run free from the defensive backs who remained in the backfield. In an instant, Eddie put on the brakes, turned, and tossed the ball back to Chava. Chava cocked his arm and unleashed a missile.

The ball spiraled perfectly through the air forty yards downfield into Anthony's waiting hands. He cradled the ball, turned on the jets, and ran the final twenty yards for a touchdown.

The whole team was thrilled. The game had been one of their best all season. Riley was excited about the win too, and she could hardly believe she was on a team with such amazing athletes, but she still didn't quite have her kicking down. She made two solid field goals against Park but missed a couple of easy extra points. She was still having a hard time deciding on the right motion.

***

The following week, the Renegades went on the road again to take on the Central Tigers. Chava and Sean starred. Chava threw four touchdown passes and ran for another, while Sean made some great open field tackles and sacked the quarterback four times. The team won easily, but again Riley's kicking was all over the place.

Riley headed off to the locker room alone, annoyed that she wasn't improving as much as she would like. She was distracted by her own thoughts when suddenly she realized she wasn't as alone as she had thought. Sean was walking toward her, coming the opposite way down the hallway. She saw him and quickened her pace, but he did too. He just managed to beat her to the door to the girls' locker room.

"Would you get out of my way?" Riley said.

Sean leaned an arm across the doorway.

"You're lucky we won," he said. "You keep missing kicks like that and one of these nights it's going to cost us."

"I'm playing the best I can," said Riley. "Just like you."

"Ha!" Sean laughed, but it came out more like a grunt. It didn't sound as though he thought anything about it was funny. "Do you even know what you're doing out there? Do you even know how to kick a football? If I spent thirty minutes watching videos online, I could learn how to kick better than you."

Riley had had enough. She tried to push Sean out of the way.

He stood strong.

"You got cut from the soccer team, right?" Riley felt a weight drop in the pit of her stomach. Her arms, which had been pushing against Sean a moment before, dropped to her sides.

"You weren't good enough, I heard." Sean had a wicked glimmer in his eyes now. "The coach felt sorry for you, but in the end she just didn't want your dead weight on the team.

How hard is soccer anyway? You run and kick a ball into a net the size of a house."

Riley was burning inside. Her heart pounded against her chest. How dare Sean bring up the soccer team! She needed to get as far away from him as possible, and she needed to do it fast. She was about to cry, or punch him, or do something else she might regret.

"Move!" was all she could get herself to say.

Sean finally stepped aside. "Do us all a favor," he said. "Stop wasting everybody's time pretending you can do something you can't."

Riley pushed open the door and retreated to the quiet of the girls' locker room. She let the hot tears she had been holding back flow down her cheeks.

Chapter 11

Riley made her way through the lunch line in the school cafeteria that Friday. As usual, the place was filled with students wolfing down their food and talking frantically to friends between mouthfuls. But the buzz in the room was different, louder than normal. Riley grabbed her lunch and headed across the cafeteria to where Aisha was sitting.

"Good luck tonight!" said an energetic freshman as Riley walked past a table filled with underclassmen.

"Thanks," Riley responded.

A couple of junior guys spotted her.

"Hey Riley, are we going to beat the Jaguars tonight?" one of them asked.

"It would be the first time in twelve years," said one of their friends.

"I think we are," said Riley.

"Yeah!" the guys looked pumped. Riley shook her head and chuckled as she walked on.

She set her tray on a table and slid into the seat across from Aisha, who was working on a poster for the upcoming student council food drive.

"Need any help?" Riley asked.

Aisha mumbled a no under her breath and kept working, so Riley got to work on her spaghetti.

In a couple of minutes Aisha looked back up at her.

"Sorry," she said. "I needed to get this done so I can get it approved before we put it up." She looked around her and seemed to notice the energy in the cafeteria. "Everyone's pretty psyched. Biggest game of the season so far!"

The Renegades were facing the West Tech Jaguars. Conference champions five years running. State champs last season. Also undefeated up to this point.

"They've beaten us every year for more than a decade," said Riley.

Like the rest of the team, Riley was wearing her black game-day jersey. Aisha was sporting black and red face paint. Nearly everyone in school had black and red somewhere on their body.

"I'm a little nervous," said Riley. "I wish I was doing better. I'm still missing so many of my kicks."

"It will be all right," said Aisha. "And don't be nervous. We're all behind you one hundred percent."

Riley nodded, trying to seem reassured. "It would help if that jerk over there would start treating me like a teammate instead of an enemy." Riley nodded to a group of boys at a table over Aisha's shoulder.

Aisha turned. "Sean?"

"Yep," Riley said. "He won't lay off."

"That's harassment," said Aisha. "You need to report him to the coach or one of the counselors. He shouldn't be able to get away with that."

Suddenly another body plopped down next to Aisha. "Hey, ladies." It was Chava.

Aisha jumped with surprise.

"The energy in here is pretty awesome, wouldn't you say?" he asked. "I think this is the year we finally beat those losers from West Tech."

"For sure," said Aisha. "You're going to have a great game. I can feel it. Four touchdown passes. That's my prediction."

"What do you think, Riley?" asked Chava. "We're going to destroy the Jaguars, am I right?"

"Sure," said Riley.

"Come on," said Chava. "You can do better than that."

"She's distracted by Sean," Aisha chimed in.

"What?" said Chava. "Is he still giving you trouble? You should've told me. I can get him to leave you alone. Where is he? I'll talk to him right now." Chava stood up and scanned the cafeteria.

"No!" Riley was almost shouting. "Don't."

"Why not?" asked Chava. "He's a lightweight. He'll listen to me. Where is he?" Chava spotted Sean and began to walk toward him.

"Chava, I said no!" This time Riley *was* shouting.

A couple of people from nearby tables stopped and looked over at her. Riley blushed as Chava froze and turned back to their table.

"Please," said Riley in a quieter voice. "I don't want to make a big thing about it. I want to handle it my way."

Chava walked back over. "I feel you," he said, nodding. "You want to stand up for yourself. You don't need someone fighting your battles for you. Pride and all that, am I right?"

"Sure, we'll go with that," Riley laughed. "Just promise me you won't say anything to him or Coach."

"Promise," said Chava. "You do your thing. I won't get in your way." He looked over at a table full of teammates. "All right, ladies. Gotta go. See you on the field, Riley."

"I'll be there," she said.

Chava walked toward the guys.

"How nice that he's letting you keep your . . . pride?" said Aisha. She and Riley laughed and went back to eating their lunches.

Chapter 12

The game that night against the Jaguars was not what anyone had hoped it would be. In fact, it was a disaster. The Renegades had a promising start on defense as they stopped the Jaguars early and forced a couple of punts, but the offense wasn't getting anything on the board. They had two drives in the first quarter that were solid but didn't get them any points.

Having stalled out each time just shy of the twenty, Riley came in for field goals and missed both of them. One was a clean miss, but the other was a botched play. On that attempt, Chava mishandled the football and didn't get the hold down right away. Riley panicked and was thrown off completely. She stepped toward the ball, but because it wasn't set up on the tee like normal, she didn't even kick at it.

When Chava realized this and eventually scooped up the ball to run with it, Riley had no idea what to do. He barked orders at her to block for him, but she froze. Chava got nailed hard by a monstrous Jaguar lineman.

After that the Jaguars absolutely took it to the Renegades.

The biggest shock came in the second half after the Renegades finally managed to score their first touchdown. Riley blasted a kickoff high into the night, savoring the feeling of doing something right after her disastrous field goal attempt. She watched as the returner set up under the ball, caught it and began running forward.

Riley waited, expecting a pile of her teammates to take him down, but he exploded through the entire Renegades line of defense and was in the clear. The only thing standing between him and the end zone was Riley.

She had no clue what to do.

She had never tackled anyone. It had never come up in practice. Coach had only ever wanted her to work on her kicking.

The kick returner ran straight toward her. As she set herself and prepared for a hard tackle, the Jaguars player made a fake to his left then dashed past Riley to the right. Once she realized what happened, Riley turned and ran after him down the field. She ran as fast as she could, but the returner kept getting farther and farther away. He was too fast for her. Just like in soccer, Riley couldn't cut it trying to run down other players. The Jaguars kick returner jogged the last few yards effortlessly into the end zone.

Riley gasped for breath and watched as the Jaguars celebrated the touchdown. She looked up at the scoreboard. The Renegades were getting beaten 31–12.

Riley closed her eyes and wished for the night to be over.

* * *

The team gathered in Coach Turner's classroom after the game and waited in silence for the coaches to join them. The game had ended with the Renegades losing 35–12. It was not a great night for anybody, but Riley couldn't help feeling major responsibility for the loss. She had done next to nothing right, missing three field goals and two extra points, not to mention the botched field goal attempt and the kickoff return catastrophes. All she wanted to do was go home and crawl into bed.

Anthony broke the silence. "They were definitely the better team tonight. But we're a better team than the one that showed up for this game."

"Seriously," said Eddie. "I didn't even recognize us out there."

"Come on, guys," said Chava. "Let's not beat ourselves up. The Jaguars did enough of that to us on the field. Yes, we were bad. We had a lousy night. But the best thing we can do is put this game behind us and come back stronger next week."

Sean stood up. "It would've been a whole

lot different if we had a kicker." All eyes went to him.

"Really, Sean?" said Chava. "That's a dumb thing to say."

"I'm telling you," said Sean. "She cost us the game tonight. It was her fault we lost."

"That's ridiculous," said Eddie. "We all choked out there."

"Sit down, Coughlin," said Anthony.

"We win as a team and we lose as a team," said Chava. "That's always the way it is."

Riley finally spoke up. "I tried my best," she said. She hated that there was a crack in her voice, but she was determined to stand up for herself. "I'll do better next time. Sorry, guys."

"You have nothing to be sorry for," said Eddie. "All of us could have played better."

"We've got your back," said Chava. "And next time, we know you'll have ours." He turned to Sean. "Isn't that right, Coughlin?"

Sean scoffed, but at that moment Coach Turner and his assistant coaches entered the room, so Sean sat down.

Chava turned to Riley.

"You all right?" he asked.

"I'll be fine," she said.

"You are not the reason the Jaguars beat us," Chava said. "I can tell you that for sure."

Riley nodded. It felt good to hear him say it, but Riley knew that she had definitely let the team down.

Chapter 13

The next week brought another home game and continued unpredictable play from Riley. She made a thirty-eight-yard field goal, but missed a shorter one and came up empty on two of the extra points she attempted. She tried mixing up her kicking motion to correct her mistakes but only ended up making new ones. Chava had a terrible game too, throwing three interceptions and failing to pass for even one touchdown. The Renegades lost to the Fairfield Mustangs by sixteen.

It was the following week's road game against the North Rockets, however, that proved to be the worst night of the season so far. For Riley *and* the Renegades.

The Rockets were bad. Really bad. They had won only one game all season, and Riley and her teammates were counting on this game to be the one that got them back on track. On top of that, a win against the Rockets meant the Renegades would start the playoffs the following week at home, against a beatable team. A loss meant they would begin the postseason on the road, against the defending state champions, the Jaguars. The same team that had beaten them so badly just weeks before.

The team knew what was as stake. Riley expected them to come out of the gates quickly and take control of the game. But the Renegades did the exact opposite. The defense gave up two touchdowns, and the Renegades kick returner fumbled twice, giving the Rockets fabulous field position both times. To top it all off, Chava was awful. He threw two interceptions and completed just four of sixteen passes through three quarters. Eddie was the only bright spot, racking up two touchdowns and rushing for close to one hundred yards.

The amazing part of this brutal game was that in the fourth quarter the Renegades still had a shot to win. Halfway through the quarter they were down by just nine points. A successful stop by the Renegades defense forced a punt, and then, after a quality return, the Renegades had the ball on their own forty-seven yard line. Over the course of the next six plays, they rattled off one successful run after another. Their offensive lineman manhandled the Rockets defense and absolutely owned the line of scrimmage. At the twelve yard line, Chava faked a handoff up the middle and then tossed the ball to Eddie, who scooted around the corner and ended up easily in the end zone.

Then it was Riley's turn. She lined up for the extra point with her heart racing. She knew how much the team needed her to make the kick and adrenaline was coursing through her body. The ball snapped perfectly into Chava's outstretched hands and he placed it on the tee as Riley made her way forward.

Solid contact. The kick was good.

Riley's extra point brought the score to 23–21.

She smiled to herself as she jogged off the field, but she knew they weren't out of the woods yet. With only three minutes to play, the Renegades would have to stop the Rockets' offense if they had any chance to win.

Riley watched from the sidelines, feeling the tension in her teammates around her. The defense stepped up and forced the Rockets to punt the ball after a three and out. Just what the team needed.

Riley knew the game might rest on her shoulders. A field goal would give the Renegades a one-point lead and quite possibly the victory. She paced on the sideline waiting for her opportunity.

On their final drive, the Renegades used all of their might to drive the ball to the Rockets' fifteen yard line. With time about to expire, Coach Turner made his decision.

"Field goal!" he shouted.

Sean was standing next to Riley. "You better make it," he said. "You better not let us down."

Riley didn't even look at Sean as she jogged onto the field, but his words bounced around in her head.

Chava greeted her. "We've got this," he said. "Let's put the rest of this game behind us and win."

"Agreed." Riley took a couple breaths, but she couldn't completely shake Sean's taunt. She thought about what she needed to do. Not only about her last successful field goal, but also about the earlier kicks she had missed that day and tried to figure out what went wrong.

With no more time to think about it, she retreated backward and sideways to her spot. She stared intently at the ball, picturing it heading in the direction it needed to travel. She could hear the opposing fans shouting behind her. This was it. Victory time.

The ball was snapped.

Chava put down the hold.

Riley stepped toward the ball and kicked. *Thwack!*

She had dug her toe into the turf before making contact with the ball. She knew right away that she'd missed. She hardly even needed to look.

The ball traveled just four or five feet off the ground and slammed into the back of one of the Renegades lineman. It bounced sideways and was swallowed up by a Rockets player who dove on top of it. Riley heard the whistles of the referees and looked up at the clock.

Time was up.

The game was over. They had lost.

She had lost.

Chapter 14

"**W**hat was it like after the game?" asked Aisha. She and Riley were sitting together at their favorite coffee place. It was Saturday morning, the day after the loss to the Rockets.

"Awful," said Riley.

"Did Sean blame you again?"

"Pretty much everybody blamed me," said Riley.

"I don't believe that," said Aisha.

"It's true," said Riley. "Even Chava couldn't look me in the eye." She took a deep breath. "And you know they're right, don't you?"

"Stop it."

Riley took a long drink from her cup. "Maybe it was a mistake for me to try to play football."

Aisha crossed her arms in front of her and gave Riley a sideways look.

"What?" said Riley. "I'm not good enough. That's obvious. I'm just dead weight."

"So you're a quitter now," said Aisha.

"Maybe."

"I see," said Aisha. "The girl who wouldn't let me quit soccer when we were little even when I cried about how bad I was all summer. The girl who practically forced me to be a candidate for student council. That same girl is going to quit football because she missed a couple of kicks. How does that make sense?" Aisha sounded annoyed.

"It was more than a couple," said Riley.

Aisha sighed. "What do you expect from me?"

"You could support me instead of criticizing," said Riley.

"I *am* supporting you," said Aisha irritably. "Because I know quitting would be a mistake for you. Remember how you felt when you got cut from the soccer team? Remember how disappointed you were? But what did you do? You put it behind you and you learned how to play football." She said it again with extra emphasis. "Football!"

"It's just kicking," said Riley.

Aisha cocked her head and glared at Riley. "Are you going to let me finish?"

Riley sighed. "Go on."

"You took the talent you had and put it to use in a completely different way," said Aisha. "And, in case you need reminding, you're really good at football. Like, setting-a-conference-record good."

"Stop," said Riley. "I get it already."

"Good," Aisha said, taking a sip of her tea.

Riley let out a deep breath. "You're right. Quitting now would be the wrong choice."

"Yep."

"I've made it this far," Riley said. "I need to stick with it. If nothing else, I want to show Sean that he can't get to me—and show everyone that I do belong on this team."

"That's what I'm talking about," said Aisha.

"This could be our final game," Riley said.

"I'm going to make sure I do everything I can to help us win."

"There you go," said Aisha.

"I'll practice all weekend! And I won't stop until my leg falls off."

"That might be a little extreme." Aisha laughed.

"Are you sure you're not mad at me?" asked Riley.

"No," said Aisha. "That was fun. It's about time I turn the tables and get on your case for a change."

"Feels good, doesn't it?"

Aisha leaned back in her chair. "It does."

Chapter 15

After she left the coffee shop, Riley did
exactly what she had done the day of tryouts
months earlier. She grabbed her dad's football
supplies and made her way to the field at the
park. She was determined to get back to the
basics and learn to become a great kicker
before the season was over and it was too late.

So that afternoon she kicked. And she
kicked and she kicked, blasting balls toward
the uprights and looking for the secret formula
to make herself better. Over and over again,
Riley set herself, stepped forward, planted her
left foot and kicked. Over and over again. She

tried different kicking motions. She altered the location of her plant foot, she tried changing the angle of her backswing, and she worked to increase her foot speed. She tried everything she could think of, looking for that just-right combination of moves.

Riley wanted to believe she was getting better, but she wasn't sure if this was true. She was still missing a lot.

She grabbed a water bottle out of the ball bag and sat down for a breather. It was then that she noticed somebody walking toward her. As the person got closer she saw that it was Chava.

"Mind if I join you?" he asked, still about twenty yards away.

"What are you doing here?" Riley blurted back, but then wondered if her question sounded rude. "No, I don't mind."

Chava walked over and sat down across from her. "Are your kicks getting any better?"

"Not really," said Riley.

"That's too bad," he said. "We're going to need you against the Jaguars."

"Are you just here to put more pressure on me? Because I really don't need—"

"I ran into Aisha and she told me where I could find you." Chava motioned for her water bottle. Riley tossed it to him and he tipped his head back for a long drink. He threw it back to her and smiled.

"So, I've been watching you." Chava's comment hung awkwardly in the air.

"Wait, what?" Riley glanced out at the park around her, spotting trees and bushes that could have acted as hiding places. "For how long?"

"Not long." Chava laughed. "I'm not a stalker or anything."

"That's good." Riley laughed too.

"I think I can help you," he said.

"Oh really," said Riley.

"You've played basketball, right?"

"Yeah."

"And you've shot free throws?" asked Chava.

"Of course."

"Let me ask you this," he said. "Do you use the same routine every time you shoot a free throw?"

"Sure," said Riley. "Everybody develops their own unique free throw style."

"That's right," said Chava. He waited in silence, looking at her and smiling.

"Your point?" asked Riley.

"Kicking can't be that different from shooting a free throw," he said. "It's just you and the ball, and it's mastering the perfect form and doing it the same every time until you get it down."

"Makes sense, I guess." Riley thought about it, going through her free throw routine in her mind.

"I've watched you," he said.

"Haven't we already established that?" Riley asked sarcastically.

Chava laughed again. "I mean all season. Not just today. You're hesitant. When you kick it seems like your motion is different every time."

"I'm trying to figure out what works," she said.

"It works when you get it through the uprights. Besides, it's too late to keep trying new motions," said Chava. "You need to kick it and be confident. Everything else will follow."

Riley threw her water bottle into the bag, grabbed a football, and stood up. "You know, you're pretty smart."

"You too," said Chava.

"You want to know something else?" asked Riley.

"Shoot."

"I've been watching you too." Riley spun the ball in her hand.

"Is that right?" he asked.

"I know why you're in a slump," she said.

He paused for a second. "I'm in a slump?" he asked. "Is that what people are saying?"

"You're guiding the ball," said Riley. "You're trying to guide the football to your target instead of just letting loose and throwing it."

Chava nodded his head in a way that seemed to say he was impressed. "Is that right?"

"I'll make you a deal," said Riley. "You help me with my kicking and I'll help you become the quarterback you've always dreamed of being."

Chava smiled at her. "You're something else, Riley Carpenter, you know that?"

"I know," said Riley.

"I'm really glad you're on the team."

"Me too."

The two of them spent the rest of Saturday kicking and throwing. They did the same for three more hours on Sunday. By Sunday afternoon, Riley was feeling confident. She had found her routine.

Riley stood under the lights of the Jaguars' field. She looked around, checking to make sure her teammates on the kickoff squad were ready. She inhaled a long breath of cool autumn air and readied herself for the opening kickoff.

It was game night—the first game of the playoffs. The Renegades were on the road, facing the West Tech Jaguars. Their stadium was a shrine to high school football. The grass was the greenest, the bleachers were the shiniest, and the scoreboard was the biggest in the conference. It was intimidating.

Riley put the stadium out of her mind. She was ready to help her team secure an upset win and show everyone that she was a force to be reckoned with. This was not going to be her final game. This was not where her season— and her career—would end. She hoped the rest of the team felt the same way.

The shrill tone of the referee's whistle suddenly rang through the air. Riley was snapped back to the moment. Fans were cheering in anticipation as Riley raised her right arm above her head, waited for her teammates to get set, and propelled herself toward the ball.

Riley's kick made solid contact. It was a beauty. The kick returner, having underestimated Riley's strength, was forced to watch the ball soar over his head and into the end zone for a touchback—her first touchback of the season. The timing could not have been any better.

Riley's teammates congratulated her as they jogged off the field. "Great start!" said Coach Turner on the sidelines.

The first half proved to be a defensive struggle for both teams. In the first quarter, after the Renegades stopped the Jaguars on their opening possession and were successful on a number of offensive plays, Riley came in for a field goal. She blasted the ball cleanly through the uprights to give the team an early 3–0 lead. The kick was just like she had practiced it and it felt wonderful.

But the next time the Renegades got the ball, Chava threw an interception that ultimately led to three points for the Jaguars. Still, the Renegades kept fighting. Before the half, Sean came up with a huge sack and fumble recovery just as time was about to expire.

Riley was up. As the seconds ticked off the clock Riley lined up, but missed a forty-two-yard field goal. She was upset, but she knew a kick from that distance would be hard for anyone, and at least the ball had gone in the right direction. Riley shook it off. At the half, the score stood tied 3–3.

Both teams hustled off the field. Riley waited for the all-clear signal from Coach

Turner then stepped inside the boys' locker room. She noticed Chava sitting alone, his face toward the floor. She walked over and sat beside him.

"We've got this," Riley said to him. "Get out of your head. Have some fun out there."

"Let me guess? I'm guiding the ball," he said with a smile.

"A little bit," she admitted.

"And I should just reach back and throw it—isn't that what you told me?" Chava asked.

"Something like that," she said.

"Okay, Coach," he said. "I'll give it a shot."

***

The Renegades got the ball to open the second half. On first down, Coach called a pass play. Chava took the snap and dropped back into the pocket. The offensive lineman protected him well, giving Chava plenty of time to survey the field and look for an open man.

Three receivers streaked down the field. Two of them did routes cutting into the middle of the field, but Anthony simply turned on the jets and ran. He flew straight up the field near the left sideline. Chava spotted him. He reached the football far behind his head, dug his back foot into the ground and unleashed a missile.

The ball fell perfectly into Anthony's arms. The defensive back in pursuit dove at his ankles but missed as Anthony dashed the final thirty yards into the end zone.

"Yes!" Riley jumped up and down on the sidelines. Her teammates erupted in cheers on either side of her.

"Extra point!" yelled Coach Turner.

Riley sprinted onto the field. The guys were still celebrating the touchdown.

"Excellent throw!" Riley shouted to Chava.

"I didn't guide it."

"No, you didn't," said Riley.

"You're going to take credit for that one, aren't you?" he asked.

"Of course," said Riley.

"Get back there and kick," Chava said, laughing.

Riley smiled and stepped into her spot. A

few seconds later, the ball was snapped and Riley did exactly what she had done the whole weekend with Chava. She stepped forward, planted her left foot, and let her right leg swing forward in a perfect arc. Riley knew she had done it.

She nailed the perfect extra point through the shiny, yellow uprights of Jaguars Stadium. Not even a corner kick had ever felt so good.

The Renegades never looked back after that. Chava went on to throw two more touchdowns, the defense stood strong when it mattered, and as the seconds ticked down, Riley, Chava, and the rest of the Renegades sealed the victory over the Jaguars, winning the game 26–10.

As the players celebrated on the field, Riley caught up with Chava.

"We did it!" She nearly knocked him over with a giant bear hug.

"We beat the Jaguars! Nobody thought we could do it!" he shouted into the night. "Unbelievable!"

"You played great, Chava," Riley said.

"Thanks," he said.

The two of them stood in silence, soaking up the win and watching their teammates hug and high-five around them.

"I'm a pretty good coach," Chava finally said.

"How do you mean?" Riley asked with a smile.

"I just spent two days showing you how to kick and now look at you," he said. "You're a superstar."

She shoved him. "Yeah, that's right. I couldn't have done it without you." Riley thought for a second. "I guess the same goes for me."

"Yeah?"

"I'm single-handedly responsible for getting you out of your funk," said Riley. "I taught you how to throw a football again. You had absolutely nothing to do with it."

Chava smiled. "How about this? We're a team, you and me. I make you better and you make me better. Together there's no saying how good we can be."

"I like the sound of that," said Riley. Then, with a grin, she added, "As long as I get all the credit."

Chava laughed. "Never!"

Their teammates continued to jump around them. Riley hoped this would be the first of many postseason victories.

"We're going to keep this rolling, right?" said Riley.

"All the way through the conference finals," said Chava.

"All the way to the state title is what I'm talking about!" said Riley.

Chava wrapped an arm around her shoulder pads. "Sounds about right to me."

Check out all
the GRIDIRON Books

GRIDIRON
THE CLUTCH
PAUL HOBLIN

GRIDIRON
THE EXTRA POINT
CHRIS KREIE

GRIDIRON
FALSE START
PAUL HOBLIN

GRIDIRON
THE LATE HIT
K. R. COLEMAN

GRIDIRON
SHOWDOWN
K. R. COLEMAN

GRIDIRON
SIGNING DAY
K. R. COLEMAN

Leave it all on the field!

Check out all the titles in the

bOUNCE

Collection

STEP UP YOUR GAME

Chris Kreie is an elementary teacher and lives in Minnesota with his wife and two children. He played football until 9th grade when he stopped to focus on basketball, his favorite sport. Now he enjoys biking, traveling, hiking, and spending time at his family's cabin.